Sandy Creek
122 Fifth Avenue
New York, NY 10011

ISBN-13: 978-1-4351-2358-8

Printed and bound in China

1 3 5 7 9 10 8 6 4 2

"Welcome to Agrabah, city of mystery. Look at this—it is no ordinary lamp. It once changed the course of a young man's life. A young man who, like this lamp, was more than what he seemed—a Diamond in the Rough. Perhaps you would like to hear the tale? It begins on a dark night where a dark man waits with a dark purpose. . . ."

In the vast Arabian desert, a horseman named Jafar waited in the moonlight. Suddenly, a thief named Gazeem appeared.

"You are late!" growled Jafar.

"A thousand apologies," Gazeem replied. He handed Jafar what he was waiting for—half of a golden scarab medallion. Jafar pulled the other half of the medallion from his robe. As the pieces were brought together, the scarab glowed—and took off like a rocket!

Jafar and Gazeem followed the soaring scarab until it crashed into a dune. Suddenly, the sand rose up in the shape of a huge tiger's head. Its mouth opened, revealing the entrance to . . .

"The Cave of Wonders!" Jafar whispered in awe. He turned to Gazeem. "Now—bring me the lamp!"

As Gazeem walked toward the cave, a booming voice stopped him: "Only one may enter here, one whose worth is far within—the Diamond in the Rough!"

The thief slowly stepped into the tiger's mouth—and its jaws slammed shut!

"What are we going to do now?" Iago, Jafar's parrot, asked.

"I must find this . . . Diamond in the Rough," Jafar declared.

The next morning, a young man named Aladdin and his
monkey, Abu, raced through the bustling marketplace of Agrabah.
"Stop, thief!" the Sultan's guards called as they chased them.
"All this . . . for a loaf of bread?" Aladdin cried as he leaped off
a roof, swung from a clothes line, and dodged swords to escape.

"And now we feast," Aladdin told Abu as they sat down to eat their first meal in days. But Aladdin realized that there were others worse off than he, and he gave the bread to a couple of hungry children. The two friends went home with empty bellies.

"Someday, Abu, things are going to change," Aladdin said as he stared out at the Sultan's palace. "We'll be rich . . . and never have any problems at all."

Meanwhile, in the palace, Princess Jasmine was very unhappy. Her father, the Sultan, wanted her to marry a snooty prince—in three days time!

"It's the law," he told Jasmine. "You're a princess."

"Then maybe I don't want to be a princess anymore," she replied as she patted her tiger, Rajah. "If I do marry, I want it to be for love."

"I've never even been outside the palace walls," Jasmine said sadly as she looked at all her pet canaries. Then she set the caged birds free!

The Sultan was at his wits' end! He called upon his most trusted advisor for help.

"Jafar, I am in desperate need of your wisdom," the Sultan pleaded. "Jasmine refuses to choose a husband."

"Perhaps I can devise a solution," Jafar said. "But it would require the use of the mystic blue diamond."

The Sultan did not want to give up his cherished ring. But Jafar used his snake staff to hypnotize him!

By the time the sun set, Jasmine had decided to run away.

"I can't stay here and have my life lived for me," she told Rajah. "I'll miss you." Then she climbed over the palace wall.

On the other side, Jasmine suddenly found herself alone in a new world—Agrabah's bustling marketplace.

The beautiful princess quickly caught the attention of Aladdin, and he began to watch her.

Seeing a hungry child, Jasmine plucked an apple from a fruit stand and gave it to him.

"You'd better be able to pay for that!" bellowed the huge fruit seller.

"P-pay?" Jasmine stammered. "I don't have any money!"

    Suddenly, Aladdin appeared and stepped in front of the angry fruit seller.

    "Oh, thank you, kind sir! I'm so glad you found her," he gushed, thinking quickly. "She's my sister. She's a little crazy!"

    Then Aladdin turned to Jasmine. "Come along, sis!" he said, taking the princess's hand. "I'll take you to see the doctor now."

Back at the palace, Jafar climbed a secret staircase to his tower laboratory. He placed the Sultan's ring inside a strange device that looked like an hourglass. Suddenly, lightning flashed—and the sands began to swirl and sparkle!

"Sands of time, reveal to me the one who can enter the cave!" Jafar demanded. An image of Aladdin appeared inside the hourglass. "There he is—my Diamond in the Rough!"

Jafar quickly ordered the Sultan's guards to find the young man and bring him to the palace.

"So, where are you from?" Aladdin asked, leading Jasmine to his rooftop home.

"I ran away," Jasmine answered with a sigh. "My father is forcing me to get married."

"That's awful," Aladdin agreed.

Just then, the palace guards swarmed up to Aladdin's hiding place. Aladdin and Jasmine tried to run away but were quickly captured.

"Just keep running into each other, don't we, street rat?" the captain of the guards said.

"Unhand him!" Jasmine cried, throwing back her hood. "By order of the Princess."

"Princess Jasmine!" gasped the surprised palace guards.

"The Princess?" gasped the surprised Aladdin.

"My orders come from Jafar," said the captain of the guards. "You will have to take it up with him."

"Believe me, I will!" Jasmine said.

At the palace, Jasmine ordered Jafar to release Aladdin.
"Sadly, the boy's sentence has already been carried
out," Jafar lied. "Death—by beheading."
    "No. How could you?" Jasmine wept as she
ran off.

Locked away in a dungeon, Aladdin could think only of the beautiful princess he would never see again. Luckily, Abu showed up and unchained him.

Suddenly, an old prisoner stepped out from the shadows. "There is a cave filled with treasure," he whispered. "Treasure enough to impress your princess."

Aladdin was intrigued by the story and followed the old prisoner through a secret passage and into the desert.

Soon he and Abu found themselves standing before the Cave of Wonders! The tiger let Aladdin pass—but instructed him not to touch any of the treasure, only the lamp.

"Fetch me the lamp, and you shall have your reward," the old man promised.

Through the mouth of the cave, Aladdin and Abu followed the steep steps down, down, down . . .

. . . until they found a huge chamber filled with mounds of golden treasure!

"Just a handful of this stuff would make me richer than the Sultan!" Aladdin exclaimed.

Abu reached for a glittering ruby.

"Don't touch anything!" Aladdin warned Abu. "We've gotta find that lamp."

Suddenly, Abu felt something tap him on the shoulder. It was a Magic Carpet!

"Maybe you can help us?" Aladdin asked the carpet. "We're trying to find this lamp."

The friendly Magic Carpet happily led Aladdin and Abu into another chamber. At the top of a massive stone staircase, Aladdin found the golden lamp resting on an altar.

Just as Aladdin reached for the lamp, Abu spotted a glittering jewel in the hands of a golden idol. The Magic Carpet tried to stop the greedy monkey, but Abu grabbed the gem.

The ground began to tremble. Then the voice of the cave spoke: "You have touched the forbidden treasure! You shall never see the light of day again!"

As the cavern began to crumble around them, Aladdin and Abu
leaped aboard the flying carpet. A sea of molten lava raced after
them as they flew toward the opening of the cave.

"Help me out!" Aladdin called as he clung to the crumbling edge of the cave. "I can't hold on!"

"First give me the lamp!" the old prisoner called back.

The minute Aladdin handed over the lamp, the old man revealed himself—he was Jafar!

The villain laughed as he dropped Aladdin back into the collapsing cave! Abu attacked Jafar, but the monkey was thrown back down as well.

"It's mine!" Jafar shrieked as he reached into his robe for the lamp—but it was gone! "Nooo!" he cried.

Inside the Cave of Wonders, it was silent as a tomb.

"We're trapped!" Aladdin cried in despair. But Abu just held out his paw and smiled.

"The lamp!" Aladdin exclaimed. The monkey had snatched it back when he attacked Jafar.

Aladdin looked at the golden lamp, trying to figure out what was so special about it. "I think there's something written here, but it's hard to make out." He rubbed the lamp to clean some of the dust off.

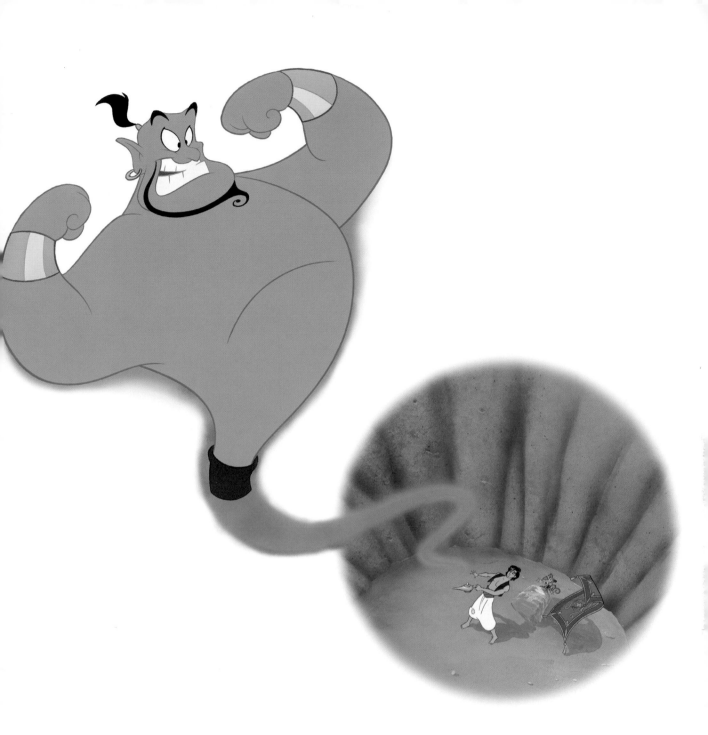

The lamp began to glow. Then a towering cloud of smoke poured from the spout—and took the form of a blue giant!

"Say, you're a lot smaller than my last master," the giant said, looking down at Aladdin.

Aladdin couldn't believe that he had his very own genie! "You're going to grant me any three wishes I want?"

Aladdin didn't want to waste a wish, so he tricked the Genie into transporting them out of the cave.

"How about that!" the Genie bragged as they all soared over the desert on the Magic Carpet.

"What is it you want most?" the Genie asked, offering Aladdin the first of his three wishes.

"Can you make me a prince?" Aladdin asked. He wanted to impress Princess Jasmine.

"Hang on to your turban, kid!" the Genie shouted. "We're gonna make you a star!"

Meanwhile, Jafar was desperate to become Sultan. But without the magic lamp to help him, he had to come up with a new plan. Whoever married Princess Jasmine would be the new Sultan. So the villain used his snake staff to hypnotize the Sultan. "You will order the Princess to marry me!" Jafar commanded.

Back in the desert, the Genie was putting the finishing touches to the new prince. Aladdin was dressed from head to toe in royal robes. Then the Genie turned Abu into a huge elephant, and Aladdin rode right into the palace courtyard—disguised as Prince Ali Ababwa!

Trumpets blared, and the doors to the palace were thrown open.
"Your Majesty, I have journeyed from afar to seek your
daughter's hand in marriage," Aladdin announced. The Sultan
was thrilled! But Jasmine thought Aladdin was just another
snooty prince.

"I am not a prize to be won!" Jasmine shouted as she stormed
out of the throne room.

To win Jasmine's heart, Aladdin sneaked up to her balcony on his Magic Carpet.

"Princess Jasmine, please give me a chance," Aladdin pleaded. Then he invited her on a moonlight ride. Jasmine realized that Prince Ali was really the young man she had met in the marketplace. By the end of the night, Aladdin and Jasmine had fallen in love!

Jafar knew he had to get rid of Prince Ali. So he ordered his guards to chain Aladdin up—and throw him into the sea!

Luckily, the Genie was nearby and Aladdin used his second wish to save himself.

"Don't scare me like that, kid," the Genie said as he unchained his master.

Aladdin raced to the palace on his Magic Carpet—
just before the Sultan ordered Jasmine to marry Jafar!
   "Your Highness, Jafar has been controlling you with this!"
Aladdin cried as he smashed the snake staff.
   "Traitor!" the Sultan cried. But before the guards could arrest
Jafar, the villain escaped.

Later, hiding in his laboratory, Jafar plotted.

"Prince Ali is nothing more than Aladdin!" he said. "He has the lamp!"

At dawn the next morning, Iago crept into Aladdin's room and stole the lamp.

At last Jafar had the lamp! Eagerly, he rubbed it, and the Genie appeared.

"I am your master now!" Jafar bellowed. "I wish to rule . . . as Sultan!"

The Genie was powerless to resist.

"Genie, no!" Aladdin screamed as Jafar took over the palace.
"Sorry, kid," the Genie said. "I've got a new master now."
Then Jafar made his second wish—to become a powerful sorcerer!

Jafar used his evil sorcery to banish Aladdin to the snowy ends of the earth! Luckily, Abu and the Magic Carpet were still with him.

"Now, back to Agrabah!" Aladdin cried as they sped off on the Magic Carpet.

Back at the palace, the poor Sultan was hanging from the ceiling of his throne room like a marionette. And Jasmine was Jafar's slave!

Jafar was so busy enjoying his power, he didn't notice Aladdin sneaking into the throne room. Just as Aladdin reached for the magic lamp, Jafar saw his reflection in Jasmine's tiara.

"How many times do I have to kill you, boy!" the villain shrieked as he fired his snake staff at Aladdin.

Jasmine ran to help her hero.

"Princess, your time is up!" Jafar said, trapping Jasmine in a huge hourglass.

"You cowardly snake!" Aladdin shouted.

"Snake, am I?" Jafar hissed. The villain turned himself into a gigantic cobra!

"The Genie has more power than you'll ever have!" Aladdin taunted.

So the power-hungry Jafar used his last wish to become a genie.

But the villain forgot one important detail—all genies must live within a lamp.

"Noooo!" Jafar cried as he was imprisoned inside a magic lamp—forever!

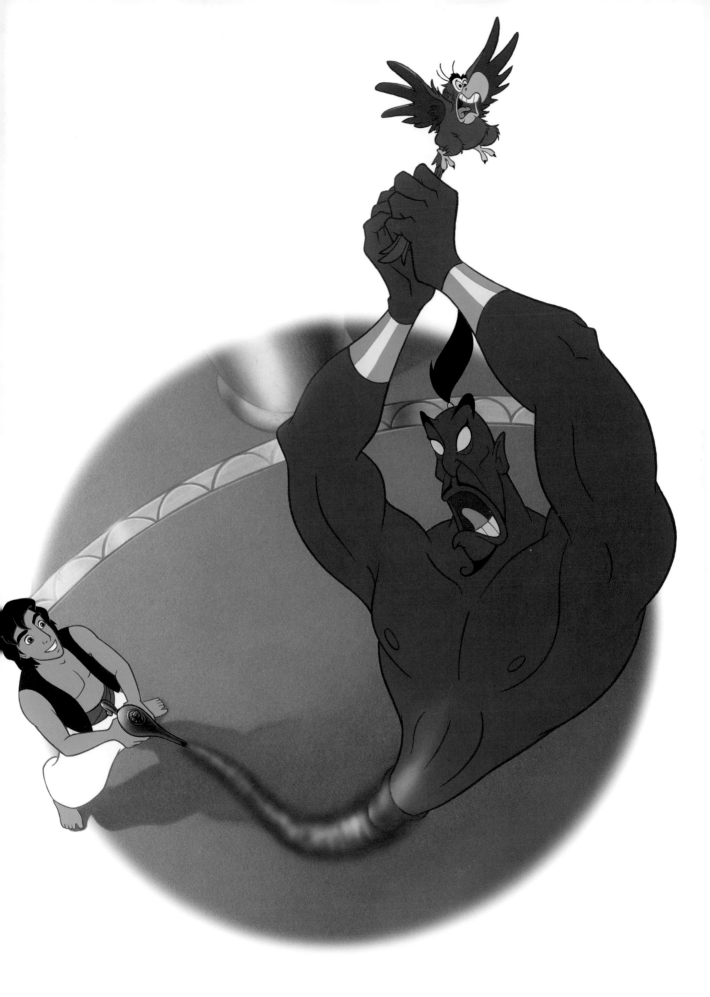

Aladdin used his third and final wish to set the Genie free. And the Sultan changed the law so that Princess Jasmine could marry anyone she chose.

"I choose you, Aladdin," Jasmine said as she kissed her prince. And they all lived happily ever after!

The End